The Heart of the Lion

Pete & Mary Watson

Best Wishes!
Pete Watson

Shenanigan Books

129 West End Ave. Summit, New Jersey   07901

Inquiries should be addressed to Shenanigan Books, 129 West End Ave., Summit New Jersey, 07901.
Printed in China
The text type is Avenier Medium.

Library of Congress Control Number: 2004099573

ISBN: 0-9726614-1-7

For Yampabou, whose name in Gourma means "Gift from God" – PW
For all who are brave enough to follow their heart – MW

ELEPHANTS

The elephants are walking, three silhouettes...hooked trunk to tail, the way they connect in a parade.

They're a trademark, I think. They're on pencils and rulers and notebooks and such...even the eraser our teacher uses to squash scorpions on the wall.

I'd like to know if a scorpion can sting through the skin of an elephant. Or a hippopotamus. Or sneakers like the ones I'm wearing.

My father doesn't think so.

"Just remember to shake out your shoes in the morning," he tells me. "That's where scorpions like to hide."

My mother stops at the table where I sit and looks at the notebook with the elephants on it. "Is this for school?" she asks.

"Yes," I say. "We have to keep a journal."

A moth flies too close to the flame of my lamp and falls to the bottom with the others.

"Why don't you clean that out?" she says. "There must be a hundred of them in there."

"Forty-seven," I say.

Then I open the notebook and begin to write.

Kᴘɪʟᴀᴅᴏᴜ

Far from the village, on the edge of a cornfield, we wait for the parrots to come. They are coming to eat Yampabou's corn, and Yampabou has asked me to help him chase them away. It is early morning, and it is still dark.

"The cornfield is big," I say to Yampabou. "How will we chase them all?"

"We will run," he says. "And we will yell."

The corn rustles and there is a monstrous cough.

"It is Kpiladou!" Yampabou whispers. "He comes to eat the corn also!"

Yampabou finds the path of trampled, half eaten corn. We follow it through the cornfield amidst the flutters of arriving birds. Soon there are hundreds, perhaps thousands of parrots in the shadowy sky.

Yampabou stops and carefully crouches to the ground. He sets the lamp inside a giant footprint and turns to me, astonished.

"He is gone!" he declares. "His path ends, here, where we stand!"

"Impossible!" I say.

Yampabou laughs softly. He is Gourma, so his teeth are filed into points. In the lamplight, he reminds me of a jack-o-lantern.

"It will be said in the village that the parrots have outsmarted the farmers and carried Hippopotamus back to his river!"

"You're joking!" I declare. "You cannot possibly believe that!"

"I am not joking," he says. "You will find Kpiladou there now...swimming in the river, his belly full of my corn."

I touch the footprint with my hand. It is cool and damp.

Yampabou

    I am waiting for Yampabou. He will come barefoot, with his lamp, to teach me things about his village.

    He does not seem to care that I am unable to grow a cornfield, or balance bundles on my head, or understand how birds can move a hippopotamus. He finds our differences quite amusing.

    Without Yampabou, I am lost in a world of mysteries and magic...among people who eat the hearts of lions.

The Hunters

Along the path to the river, I met 3 little boys roasting a mouse.

The oldest had killed the mouse. Another held the mouse on a stick and turned it over a fire. The youngest carefully fed twigs into the fire.

The boys were squatting, sitting back on their heels with their arms up over their knees the way grown men do when they roast pieces of hedgehog or antelope or wild boar.

When the mouse was cooked, the boys divided it up. The one who caught it got the head. The next one got the body. The youngest got the feet and the tail.

The young hunters offered me some of their meat, because it is the custom to share whatever you have, even if you have very little.

Scorpion Man

In the village where I live, there is someone I call scorpion man.

He is crazy, I think. He keeps a scorpion in a little matchbox, and whenever he sees me coming he takes it out and and puts it on his tongue. Then he closes his mouth so the scorpion is inside, stinger and all.

He rolls his eyes and throws his head from side to side, moaning, as though he is being stung to death. Then he opens his mouth again, and the scorpion walks out to the end of his tongue and drops into the matchbox.

"Why doesn't it sting him?" I ask Yampabou when we are working in the garden.

Yampabou stops and places his hoe on his shoulder. "He cannot be stung!" he answers. "He is someone who has been given power over the scorpion...so that if you are stung, you can find help."

"But who would want the help of a crazy man?" I ask.

Yampabou laughs. "If you are stung by a scorpion, my friend, you will run to his house and pray that he is there. And if you find him, you will not ask if he is crazy. You will beg for his cure."

Kokeeda

Seku the blacksmith keeps his chickens in a little mud coop behind his house. There the roots of a giant baobab tree weave over the rocks, making tunnels and holes where the chickens find beetles and other good things to eat.

Yesterday, Kokeeda hid in the baobab's roots and waited for the chickens to come. But as fate would have it, the birds stayed inside their coop all day and the snake waited in vain.

Sometime during the night, the snake's hunger got the better of him and he entered the coop through the little hole the chickens use as a door. He swallowed four of the poor birds before Seku was awakened by the squawking and came running with an axe. He found the snake struggling to escape, his head poking out the door, his body stuck inside...too swollen with chickens to pass through.

In the morning, Seku invited everyone to his house for a feast that included four roasted chickens and the meat of Kokeeda.

The chickens were cooked whole and arranged in the same order they were found inside Kokeeda's belly. Seku said a prayer of thanksgiving for the meat that would be shared by all, and then gave the head of the snake to Bundari, the medicine man.

The feast lasted long into the night, when the moon was high overhead and the mockingbird sang in the branches of the great baobab tree.

BUTTERFLY BOY

Near the well in Dambouti, there is a crippled boy who sells butterflies. He has hundreds of them, all colors and shapes, all carefully pressed and arranged on the leaves of banana trees.

He tells me that when he has sold enough butterflies, he will go to the hospital and pay doctors to make him well.

"Who buys your butterflies?" I ask him.

"Merchants," he replies, "the ones who also buy ivory and the skins of animals."

Then he adds, "Friend, do you know the artists who paint with the wings of butterflies?"

"No," I say. "No."

His hand is thin and twisted like his legs. But he somehow lifts it and points to the road. "They live far away by the sea," he says. "They wait for merchants to bring them my butterflies."

Last night I asked Yampabou about the butterflies.

"Oh yes," he says, "they are made into paintings for tourists to buy. The lion, the elephant, the monkey, the chameleon...all have been painted with the wings of Yarou's butterflies."

"Painted?" I ask.

"Yes. That is to say, the wings are detached and cut into pieces. Then they are glued onto paper to form whatever picture the artist desires."

"You mean a mosaic," I say. "Yes, I see."

But soon I do not see, and I must ask Yampabou another question. "How does the boy catch the butterflies? He cannot walk. He can barely lift his hand...."

"My friend," he says smiling, "The butterflies come willingly to the place where he sits, as though he were the nectar they seek. And in the moment when they have freed him of his chains, they will fly from the paintings that hold them and dance again in the fields."

THE PRISONER

  In front of the Tanguieta store, there is a baboon chained to a mango tree. He has been there a long time, I think, because his teeth are very yellow from smoking cigarettes thrown to him by tourists and safari men.

  They throw him other things, too – bottle caps, candy wrappers, bits of food. These are his treasures, which he keeps in a hole in the tree. He guards them jealously, chasing anyone who enters the little circle of sand that is his home...and his prison.

  Once he caught a boy trying to steal his treasures. He grabbed him as he ran and bit off his thumb. Now the thumb is in there, too. Or at least the bones from it.

Today I went to Tanguieta by bush taxi to get packages at the post office. As we rumbled past the side street where the baboon is chained, I saw children teasing him the way they always do. They had lured him to the end of his chain with a cola nut. One was out behind, sneaking toward his tree.

Leaving Tanguieta, we passed the street again. We were going faster this time, so I didn't see it all. The baboon was running, his chain nearly taut. A child was diving, his foot nearly caught.

Then there were doorways and trees, and doorways and streets...and the rumble of the truck, and the red dust of Tanguieta rolling and roostertailing behind us.

I thought I heard a scream, but it was probably just the squeal of the tires as we rounded a bend and headed out into the bush.

The Poison Seller

In the marketplace there is a blind man who sells poison to put on arrows. It is the kind of poison that kills the prey without spoiling the meat.

When the arrow pierces the skin, the poison dissolves in the bloodstream and goes to the heart. The animal dies quickly and the hunter's work is done.

Today I watched the man sell poison to a hunter who came down from the hills. With a knife, he made a small cut in his arm so the blood trickled down to his wrist. Then he took a poison arrow and touched the blood on his wrist.

The blood turned very black, and the blackness raced up his arm toward the cut. At the last possible second, he put his finger over the cut and smiled.

The hunter was pleased and he bought the poison.

"How did he know when to stop the poison?" I asked Yampabou when we were sitting in his house that night. "He is blind!"

Yampabou shook his head at my question, the way he always does. "Does the bat need eyes in order to fly through the darkness?" he asked. "Does the lion cub open his eyes before finding his mother's milk?"

I was starting to argue with Yampabou when a moth fluttered into the kerosene lamp and fell down inside.

"Here," he said taking it out and holding it up as final proof.

"Here is a creature that could see quite well. But did it save him from the poison made for him?"

THE DOG EATERS

The people of our village say the Yawabous who live in the mountains are savages.

"They are dog eaters, my friend," says Yampabou pointing to my little brown dog, the one I call Minka. "A nice fat dog like this one will make a fine feast for those savages."

"That is terrible!" I say stroking Minka's head. "In my country, we do not eat dogs!"

"My friend," he exclaims, "we have heard that your countrymen eat the flesh of pigs...including the feet! Is that any better than eating the flesh of dogs?"

"It is different," I explain. "Pigs are raised to be eaten."

"So are dogs!" he laughs, "...among the Yawabou!"

I am angry with Yampabou. "What about you?" I ask. "Did you not tell me that you will one day kill a lion and eat its heart in order to gain its courage?"

He laughs. "It is true what you say. It is amusing, is it not...that what is forbidden for one is completely acceptable for another?"

My little dog lifts her head at the sound of wind in the leaves. I wonder if she has seen the dog buyers leaving our village with her kin tied to their ropes. Dogs too old to hunt. Dogs too old to guard Gourma houses.

MAGIC

Outside the blacksmith's shop, half buried under a heap of rusty scrap iron, there is a long, shiny slab of metal.

"Can you make me a knife from the silver metal?" I asked Seko, the blacksmith. We were inside his forge. It was a round hut with a straw roof, and dark inside except for glowing coals.

"It is useless for making knives," he said as he hammered a piece of red hot steel that he took from the coals. "When it is hot, it cannot be shaped like other metal. It melts and must be poured into molds."

"Where did it come from?" I asked.

He put his work back in the fire and pushed some hot coals over it. "It comes from go-gunu," he said holding out his arms like the wings of a bird. "My father and uncles carried it on their heads for three days, thinking it was suitable for the forge, like the metal of trucks. But it melted, of course, because it is the metal of go-gunu."

Later, we went outside and Seko got a rusty bar of metal from the scrap heap. "I will make you a good knife from truck metal," he said. "And if you wish, I will make its handle from the shiny metal of go-gunu."

Yampabou," I said when he was cutting yams to roast in the fire, "Seko is making me a knife with a handle made of go-gunu. What kind of metal is that?"

"It is airplane metal," he said. Then he laughed and said, "So you are brave like the blacksmith...and not afraid of the coffin of the dead!"

"What do you mean?" I asked.

Yampabou pointed his knife at the distant mountains. "The airplane is on top of the mountain...and its passengers with it!"

"An airplane?" I asked, "...with people inside?"

"Of course they are inside!" he laughed. "Do the dead walk away from their own coffin?"

Then he looked at me and shook his head. "You yourself do not believe in such things, so I hesitate to tell you the rest...."

"The rest of what?" I demanded.

"Very well," he said, putting the yams in the fire. "In the moment of the crash, the pilots disappeared. They were later seen among the mountain people, dining with their Chief!"

"You mean, the pilots parachuted from the plane...and left the passengers to die?"

"There were no parachutes!" he laughed. "They lived because of magic!"

Yampabou showed me the small, square pouch attached to the strip of leather that circled his waist.

"When it is time for you to go back to your country, I will give you magic like this, if you wish. Then, should an accident befall you along the way, you will disappear completely...until you are seen again, safe, among your people."

I looked out at the mountains. They were fading in the sunset like coals in a fire. I wondered if I would wear the magic pouch.

The Thief

Bundari, the medicine man, told me how to catch the thief who was taking things from our house.

"You must find the fertile eggs of Guinea hens," he said. "You will break an egg at each door and window of your house. In three days, you will catch the thief in your doorway."

I did what the medicine man said, and waited.

But towards the end of the first day, I noticed a cat near the house and I discovered that she had eaten two of my eggs. I chased her away, and when no one was looking, I replaced the eggs.

On the second day, my father noticed the egg I had hidden beneath the kitchen window. "Look," he said. "A silly Guinea hen laid her egg here...and someone stepped on it!" Then he kicked some dirt over it so it would not attract ants.

I was afraid that my chances of catching the thief were now ruined, but I did not give up hope entirely.

On the third day, I learned from our school teacher that among certain tribes, a thief who was discovered was banished from the village. The thief was required by law to leave within a day, taking with him only what he could carry on his head. The remainder of his belongings, including his house, became the property of his victim.

When I learned this, I no longer wanted to catch the thief. After school I ran to our house and collected all the eggshells I could find. Then I covered the yolks with big clumps of dirt and stomped them down.

But it was too late. At night, the thief came. I heard him enter through the kitchen window, where he upset the lamp on the table. I heard him taking the lids off the big clay pots where we stored our food. I heard him drop silverware, and I heard him break a glass.

I lay in my bed, paralyzed, not wanting to see his face or know his identity. I could think only of his last walk through the village, and his great shame. I wondered if his children were my schoolmates. I thought of them leaving the village with their parents, carrying their belongings on their heads.

When I thought that he was gone, I tiptoed to the kitchen with my flashlight to see what he had taken.

But he was not gone. He stood frozen in the light, holding a spoon and a banana.

"Su-Su!" I whispered. "You are the thief! I will tell Yampabou about you and he will sell you to tourists!"

Poor Su-Su dropped his things and covered his eyes in shame. He came to me, whimpering, and climbed up on my shoulder.

"Alright," I said petting his tiny head. "Alright. I promise not to tell them what a bad, bad monkey you've been."

THE LION

Long into the night we dig the pit where Yampabou will catch his lion. It is a long, deep pit with a column of earth in the corner where a lamp is lit.

Around the pit, men drum and sing, and women roast corn and yams.

By midnight, the pit is deep and the diggers need a rope to raise the buckets of loose dirt. By daybreak the work is done and Yampabou covers the pit with brush.

"Will you really kill the lion?" I ask him as we return to the village. "Will you roast his heart and eat it?"

Yampabou does not answer.

At the beginning of the dry season, when the desert winds blow and bushfires blacken the earth, the news came that a lion had fallen into the pit. Yampabou took the club that his father made for him and went into the bush.

"He will return at sunset with a lion's heart," his father told me. "We will prepare the feast!"

But sunset came and went, and he did not return.

Long after dark, the men went to the pit. They found Yampabou's club leaning against a nearby tree. Yampabou was in the pit, in the lamplight, chanting a strange chant. The lion was in the shadows, as though hypnotized.

Yampabou ordered the men to lower a big branch into the pit. Then he spoke to the lion. The lion jumped onto the branch and stood directly above Yampabou for a moment. Then he leapt away into the darkness.

Later, in the village, we feasted on goat meat and yams, and listened to the griot sing songs of the hunt. He sang of great, fearless hunters who had taken the hearts of lions. And of one so courageous that he set his lion free.